Transfiguration

Moisés Morán Vega

Published by Ediciones Doble A, 2024.

This is a work of fiction. Similarities to real people, places, or events are entirely coincidental.

TRANSFIGURATION

First edition. August 15, 2024.

Copyright © 2024 Moisés Morán Vega.

ISBN: 979-8227548757

Written by Moisés Morán Vega.

Angélica was reviewing the last class, reading a topic on microbiotics. She paused her reading to look at the photograph on the dresser. In it were all her cousins and Grandpa Juan, gathered around the ancient dragon tree.

She often recalled, with nostalgia, the years of her childhood spent in the village what she considered the best years of her life. Back then, the whole family would go up to Teror, a charming village in Gran Canaria, to spend the three summer months at her grandparents' house. It was a magnificent, welcoming, and familial manor house with a large central patio, where a water filter stood in one corner, its pitcher always full of fresh water, surrounded by ferns.

The patio was filled with ferns, impatiens, ivy, pothos, syngoniums, roses, thyme, mint, parsley, chamomile, oregano, several singing canaries, Bartolo the parrot, Juana the tortoise, and her sister, and the grand dragon tree, which majestically occupied the entire center of the patio. There, next to the dragon tree, Grandpa Juan would sit in the late afternoon with all his grandchildren, with a fresh cup of coffee prepared by Grandma Carmela, telling them the most incredible stories ever told of his travels across the five continents. Grandpa Juan had always been a great storyteller.

Those were undoubtedly unforgettable years. But everything changed when Grandpa passed away. When Angélica's father found a job in Las Palmas de Gran Canaria, their visits to Teror became less frequent as they permanently moved to the capital.

From then on, they only went up for the fiestas del Pino, where the whole family would gather, but always with a bittersweet feeling, as Grandpa Juan's absence filled the house;

they missed him, as he had been the life of the party and the heart of the home.

At nineteen years old, Angélica was an attractive young woman, nearly six feet tall, with dark hair, shoulder-length, black eyes, and an athletic build, making her hard to miss by most of the boys in her neighborhood and at her college. She was a solitary girl. She enjoyed and cherished her solitude. She had some friends, mostly from the last years of high school and a few from the first year of Marine Sciences.

It was in solitude where she found that special and different time that allowed her to grow inwardly. She read almost everything she could get her hands on poetry, novels, and stories. Reading was a window to the universe of knowledge that expanded within her like a nova.

However, this sought-after, not imposed, solitude did not prevent her from having a good conversation with a good friend, taking a walk along Las Canteras beach, and enjoying the soothing sound of the waves and the scent of the sea.

She didn't frequent the nightlife like other young people her age, who spent nights hopping from one party to another, with alcohol flowing freely. She preferred to stay home studying, reading a good book, or sitting in front of the computer, traveling through cyberspace, which offered her entertainment more in line with her way of being and feeling.

One of these alternatives was chatting, where she found an endless variety of characters to talk to and have fun with. She recognized that, in the jungle of the internet, it was very difficult to find interesting people, but she found them intelligent people with good conversation and much to offer.

TRANSFIGURATION

She was well aware of the dangers of chatting, and on more than one occasion, she had evaded some unscrupulous individuals who had tried to blackmail her, but she had resolved it by reporting it to the authorities, who had taken appropriate action.

She thought most men were cut from the same cloth, a pattern few had escaped since birth. They had a fixed idea in their heads not to be with one woman, as that was too tedious, but with an exponential and indistinct number of women of all ages and characteristics.

After some experiences, she had concluded that it was a matter of biology; somehow, men had it in their genes, passed down from generation to generation, and by now, it was very difficult to change.

In each chat session, she used different aliases because she didn't like being recognized. Andromeda, Arcadia, Cassandra, Harpy, Pandora, etc., were some of the different names she used when entering a chat.

She thought it was an absolute waste of time to enter the same place day after day, especially with the same alias. She never understood those characters who had spent years living in the same chat, nor did she understand the meetups, which seemed to her a substitute for the single's mixers where some people were looking for a monthly escape from imposed loneliness, to dust off and clear away the cobwebs from their genitals.

On very few occasions did she cross the invisible line of the online world, as she didn't understand or believe in these kinds of relationships, thinking they evaporated with the first rays of morning sun. Although she had crossed that line a few times to meet in person a guy who seemed interesting to her.

These encounters, most of the time, ended in an attempt, sometimes subtle, sometimes direct, to take her to bed without further ado. Only once had she allowed a guy to cross the tangible boundaries of her sexuality because that guy, aside from having good conversation and manners, made her libido levels rise uncontrollably when she first saw him, and her body was asking for a little interpersonal war.

Later, she found that the young man had other good physical attributes and knew perfectly well how, when, and for what purpose to use them.

One of the nights when she was navigating the seas of the internet, she searched for the Second Life website, which had piqued her interest after reading a report in the free city newspaper. What interested her the most was the possibility of creating a virtual character different from who she was and being able to live a second life online.

The first thing she did was research this portal. She found very interesting information on Wikipedia that gave her a fairly clear outline of what it was and the multiple possibilities the portal offered.

After gathering all the necessary data and studying it carefully, she decided to open an account and become a resident of Second Life.

She spent some time thinking about the name for her resident and, most importantly, what character she wanted to give her new personality. She spent an hour and a half mulling over, first, her new name and second, the characteristics of her new identity.

Her resident's name would be Quirina Muhindra, and her personality had to be completely different from what she was in reality. So she designed her profile, seeking her opposite traits to start working.

Once registered, she began to think about the physical characteristics of her avatar. She would be a woman of five foot seven, with short blonde hair and blue eyes. Her facial features would be those of a strong woman, very pronounced, with two visible piercings, one on her nose, another on the left side of her lower lip, and a steel cross on her right nipple. She also decided that she would always wear very tight clothing, mainly leather and lycra, which gave her an impressive look at first glance.

In this way, she built what would be her external profile in a world that was still completely unknown to her and one she would undoubtedly have to explore for some time.

After some days of doing small explorations through the virtual universe of SL cities, getting to know them firsthand, she began to search for places that matched her new identity.

She also found that she could change the color, shape, and size of her hair every day and put on or take off any outfit. One day she had a shaved head, another with spiked hair, another with two pigtails, and most of the time, a black wool hat with a golden six-pointed star in the center, which completely covered her head.

Thus, over the months, she gradually configured what would become her final image and became known in the most diverse circles of this virtual and parallel world.

Meanwhile, in real life, she continued with her life, her studies, and her few friends, but now, she locked herself in every night to travel through that unknown land with a single click of the mouse. She traveled with a completely different personality, one that she gradually adapted to over time. She felt very connected to the character she had created.

After being a resident for a little more than nine months, she decided to invest two hundred euros she had saved to pay for a Premium account and buy a plot of 4,096 square meters because she had found that in SL, you could make some money if you had imagination and time.

She had considered various types of business to set up in the space she had acquired. She knew that a considerable number of commercial ideas had worked perfectly in this virtual world and that many residents were making substantial amounts of money with imaginative businesses.

She also found that most of the world's major real-world brands had their space in Second Life because they knew money was moving there, and they couldn't miss the opportunity.

After considering and discarding more than twenty ideas to carry out, she designed a nightclub called Quimera.

She decided to launch it, and over the months, Quimera became a meeting point for many residents, whose entrance fee was about 250 Linden Dollars ($L), one dollar at the exchange rate, paid by credit card or through PayPal. The exclusive rooms with restricted access had a price of 1250 $L.

The main feature of Quirina's nightclub was that within it, all kinds of legal activities were allowed, and there was complete freedom. All were under the control of a group Quirina had gathered with special volunteers, whose only payment was free access to all the services the nightclub offered. This group of guards had the power to eject anyone who stepped out of line in Quimera with a single click.

TRANSFIGURATION

The two hundred euros she invested soon became a very profitable investment because Quimera's name spread like wildfire by word of mouth through most SL places, and the nightclub quickly became a reference point for entertainment and contact in the virtual world.

The success of her club provided her with a monthly profit of fifteen hundred euros, which she partially reinvested in enhancing her venue, and the rest she saved.

Quirina was always visible every day at her workplace, as she thought she had to control it personally. She appeared every night at the same time, at ten o'clock, although Quimera never closed, as it was open 24 hours a day.

Most clients wanted to talk to her, but it was very difficult, as she was always in an exclusive room for personal use. However, she often came down to one of the floors and talked with customers who wanted to chat, and if she found someone of special interest, she invited them to her room.

One of them, who went by the name Maliko Kundera, had been eager to talk to her for several nights.

His avatar was quite attractive, a tall, long-haired man, with dark glasses, six feet three inches tall, broad shoulders, and perfect legs. She arranged to meet him the next night in her office.

She spoke with Álvaro Zapatero, a costume designer who frequented Quimera's gay room almost every night and with whom she had a good relationship. Quirina told him she wanted an outfit for the next evening, and Álvaro, who knew her tastes perfectly, told her not to worry, that he would have it ready and send it to her account before eight o'clock in the evening.

The suit the designer made was a one-piece lycra suit, black with red and blue stripes on the sides that spectacularly accentuated her figure.

Quirina was very impressed with the design and congratulated Álvaro on his work. As a reward, she gave him a full year of free entry to any of Quimera's rooms, in addition to paying for the suit.

Maliko was punctual for the appointment, arriving at exactly ten o'clock at night. He showed up in a well-tailored blue suit, with his hair tied back in a ponytail and his beard neatly trimmed.

She watched him from her office and, without wasting any time, opened a private chat and called him, activating the voice chat.

"Maliko, you can come up now."

Her guest headed to Quirina's room.

"It seems we finally get to talk. You've been very insistent on getting this appointment with me," Quirina commented.

"It's just that I've always admired you. In a short time and with a good idea, you've managed to achieve great success," Maliko flattered her.

"More or less, there's still a lot to do, but I'm satisfied. In work, a dose of luck and opportunity is necessary."

"Just out of curiosity, do you work in the entertainment business in real life?"

"I don't talk about my private life, and besides, it's neither of your business nor does it matter what I do out there. You know that in SL, anonymity is one of the fundamental rules."

"Oh, come on, don't be like that, it's just curiosity, a way to break the ice, you know what I mean," he said, trying to apologize.

"No, I don't understand, and I don't like nosy people," Quirina replied curtly.

"Ugh, it seems I haven't started very well; you seem a bit edgy. I've just come to talk business, about making a lot of money in a very easy way."

"When money is made very easily, there's something shady behind it. Money, as you say, doesn't fall from the sky; Balzac said it: behind every great fortune, there is a crime. I hope not to have any on my shoulders; I just want to have enough work to make a living, not a gram more."

"On top of that, a cultured woman..." Maliko ironized.

"I liked *The Godfather* a lot... But who says I'm a woman and not a man? Don't forget I'm just an avatar in a fictional world, where we can all be whatever we want, bringing out from deep within us what we are not in the real world, bringing it here and giving it life."

"I think you take this very seriously; for me, it's just a place where it seems you can do good business."

"I give it the importance it has, no more, no less, and that importance I measure by the time and money I have invested. This is a place like the real world, with its same virtues and its same miseries. If you don't fight for what's yours, they'll end up taking it from you," Quirina stated.

"Well, that's what I'm here for, to talk about money... about a business," Maliko said, hesitantly.

"A business? My nightclub is thriving, it's full 24 hours a day with people from all over the world," Quirina commented with satisfaction.

"Yes, there's no doubt about it; spending a few hours here is enough to see that your idea turned out perfectly. But Quimera lacks something to take it to the top, if you know what I mean. My friends and I can help you make more money than you've ever dreamed of."

"And you and your friends have the key to total success, right?" Quirina asked sarcastically.

"Yes, it's very simple. Sex Quimera lacks sex. You know that sex is the engine that drives the world and, of course, it's the engine of Second Life; you just need to take a walk to see what I'm talking about."

"I know what you're talking about; I've spent many months exploring this world, but don't tell me stories, I know perfectly well what drives the internet, and it's not just sex. However, let me remind you that I already have sex in my club, and it's nothing other than what my clients want and desire, period. If they feel like having virtual sex, I'm not going to stop them. What they do in the VIP rooms is none of my business."

"Yes, but you're missing that little specialty touch, you know what I mean. Should I give you an example?" Maliko said.

"Don't give me examples; I know my club, and I know what I want in it. I'm not going to turn it into a dive; I don't need to. Each of my clients does what they want, and they pay for it. They know the rules, and if they break them, they're out and won't be back for a long time."

"I know some high-class prostitutes who frequent your club," Maliko countered.

"A business? My nightclub is thriving, it's full 24 hours a day with people from all over the world," Quirina commented with satisfaction.

"Yes, there's no doubt about it; spending a few hours here is enough to see that your idea turned out perfectly. But Quimera lacks something to take it to the top, if you know what I mean. My friends and I can help you make more money than you've ever dreamed of."

"And you and your friends have the key to total success, right?" Quirina asked sarcastically.

"Yes, it's very simple. Sex Quimera lacks sex. You know that sex is the engine that drives the world and, of course, it's the engine of Second Life; you just need to take a walk to see what I'm talking about."

"I know what you're talking about; I've spent many months exploring this world, but don't tell me stories, I know perfectly well what drives the internet, and it's not just sex. However, let me remind you that I already have sex in my club, and it's nothing other than what my clients want and desire, period. If they feel like having virtual sex, I'm not going to stop them. What they do in the VIP rooms is none of my business."

"Yes, but you're missing that little specialty touch, you know what I mean. Should I give you an example?" Maliko said.

"Don't give me examples; I know my club, and I know what I want in it. I'm not going to turn it into a dive; I don't need to. Each of my clients does what they want, and they pay for it. They know the rules, and if they break them, they're out and won't be back for a long time."

"I know some high-class prostitutes who frequent your club," Maliko countered.

The two hundred euros she invested soon became a very profitable investment because Quimera's name spread like wildfire by word of mouth through most SL places, and the nightclub quickly became a reference point for entertainment and contact in the virtual world.

The success of her club provided her with a monthly profit of fifteen hundred euros, which she partially reinvested in enhancing her venue, and the rest she saved.

Quirina was always visible every day at her workplace, as she thought she had to control it personally. She appeared every night at the same time, at ten o'clock, although Quimera never closed, as it was open 24 hours a day.

Most clients wanted to talk to her, but it was very difficult, as she was always in an exclusive room for personal use. However, she often came down to one of the floors and talked with customers who wanted to chat, and if she found someone of special interest, she invited them to her room.

One of them, who went by the name Maliko Kundera, had been eager to talk to her for several nights.

His avatar was quite attractive, a tall, long-haired man, with dark glasses, six feet three inches tall, broad shoulders, and perfect legs. She arranged to meet him the next night in her office.

She spoke with Álvaro Zapatero, a costume designer who frequented Quimera's gay room almost every night and with whom she had a good relationship. Quirina told him she wanted an outfit for the next evening, and Álvaro, who knew her tastes perfectly, told her not to worry, that he would have it ready and send it to her account before eight o'clock in the evening.

The suit the designer made was a one-piece lycra suit, black with red and blue stripes on the sides that spectacularly accentuated her figure.

Quirina was very impressed with the design and congratulated Álvaro on his work. As a reward, she gave him a full year of free entry to any of Quimera's rooms, in addition to paying for the suit.

Maliko was punctual for the appointment, arriving at exactly ten o'clock at night. He showed up in a well-tailored blue suit, with his hair tied back in a ponytail and his beard neatly trimmed.

She watched him from her office and, without wasting any time, opened a private chat and called him, activating the voice chat.

"Maliko, you can come up now."

Her guest headed to Quirina's room.

"It seems we finally get to talk. You've been very insistent on getting this appointment with me," Quirina commented.

"It's just that I've always admired you. In a short time and with a good idea, you've managed to achieve great success," Maliko flattered her.

"More or less, there's still a lot to do, but I'm satisfied. In work, a dose of luck and opportunity is necessary."

"Just out of curiosity, do you work in the entertainment business in real life?"

"I don't talk about my private life, and besides, it's neither of your business nor does it matter what I do out there. You know that in SL, anonymity is one of the fundamental rules."

"Oh, come on, don't be like that, it's just curio[us] to break the ice, you know what I mean," he said, [to] apologize.

"No, I don't understand, and I don't like nos[y]," Quirina replied curtly.

"Ugh, it seems I haven't started very well; you s[eem] edgy. I've just come to talk business, about making a lot [of money] in a very easy way."

"When money is made very easily, there's someth[ing] behind it. Money, as you say, doesn't fall from the sky; [I see] it: behind every great fortune, there is a crime. I hope n[ot to have] any on my shoulders; I just want to have enough work [for a] living, not a gram more."

"On top of that, a cultured woman..." Maliko ironi[zed].

"I liked *The Godfather* a lot... But who says I'm a wo[man], not a man? Don't forget I'm just an avatar in a fictio[nal world,] where we can all be whatever we want, bringing out [what is] within us what we are not in the real world, bringing it [out,] giving it life."

"I think you take this very seriously; for me, it's ju[st] where it seems you can do good business."

"I give it the importance it has, no more, no less, [an] importance I measure by the time and money I have [invested]. This is a place like the real world, with its same virtue[s,] same miseries. If you don't fight for what's yours, they'[ll be] taking it from you," Quirina stated.

"Well, that's what I'm here for, to talk about mone[y,] a business," Maliko said, hesitantly.

"I know, and they know I know, and that's enough for me. Besides, they're under control," Quirina said bluntly.

"Then you're contradicting yourself, aren't you?" Maliko said.

"Contradicting myself? No way, one thing is to allow a client to have a fling with another client, and a very different thing is to turn Quimera into a brothel. That's not the philosophy with which I founded this nightclub. Quimera is a meeting place where people come to have fun, to socialize, to get to know each other, to listen to good music played by the best DJs in the world, and even to fall in love."

"Yes, all that's fine, but I have very good contacts who will provide you with what you need for what I'm proposing; you just provide your successful club, and we'll provide the rest. A business where the money will come to you clean and easy."

"Frankly, I don't care about your contacts; I couldn't care less about the sex trade, sex for sex's sake. Your time is up; I know your proposal, and you know my answer," Quirina said bluntly.

"You could have a lot of problems if you don't accept; we can make your life miserable by sending some of our friends to mess up your business. This works like the real world; you're either with us or against us. Besides, don't think it's too difficult to find out who's behind Quirina; we have very good IT people who work very well, and we can pay you a visit in your harsh reality," Maliko threatened.

"On top of that, threats? Goodbye, idiot," and with a single click, she banned Maliko's IP.

Quirina remained thoughtful for a few moments in her office, assessing the extent of the threat as she watched Maliko disintegrate from Quimera. She gave the necessary orders to ensure Maliko never returned and reported the incident to the SL authorities to take appropriate measures, although she knew there was little they could do; Maliko would return as another avatar.

She was aware that people with very high IT skills could, given enough time and well paid, find out all the details behind an internet profile; it was just a matter of time. She had not taken the necessary precautions to hide behind an IP, knowing there were anonymous servers that provided this service, but she hadn't thought it necessary until now. But now it was too late; she was convinced they had already traced her, and she just hoped that jerk's threats would remain just that.

In Second Life, a lot of money was circulating, and money always ends up attracting the bad guys, who have very few scruples to achieve their goals. Quirina knew that, for the mafias, the line between the virtual and real worlds was very thin and could be crossed if necessary. Money always ends up breaking down ethical and moral barriers, even in the virtual world.

Quirina was aware that her nightclub had skyrocketed, that she was making a lot of money, and that her bank account was growing exponentially. Angélica spent a few seconds thinking about the conversation between her avatar and Maliko's. She reflected on the direction her second life was taking and was amazed at how easily she was using the nocturnal and street slang, but she didn't give it much importance.

She was unsure how far Maliko's intimidation could go. At that moment, the boundary between the tangible and virtual worlds was unclear to her; however, Maliko's warning had seemed very real.

TRANSFIGURATION

The next morning, she woke up feeling nostalgic because she knew something inside her was changing, and sooner or later, it would be impossible to recover it. She searched for the photo album she kept on the top shelf of her wardrobe, dusted off the accumulated dust with one hand, and opened it to the first page. There were her first photos from when she was barely two years old. She kept flipping through the pages until she reached the snapshots where she was with Grandpa Juan and all her cousins in the patio of the Teror house.

She smiled, remembering that time as a happy period. There they were, all the people who made her summers in Teror wonderful days, full of stories and adventures.

She continued looking at the old photos until she found a picture of Pepín, the altar boy of the Basilica of Teror, and couldn't help but burst out laughing, a laugh that echoed throughout the house as she remembered the incident in the bell tower. "Pepín, my friend Pepín," she thought.

She recalled how Pepín had always been crazy about her, madly in love, writing her love poems and secretly giving them to her in the square, giving her unconsecrated communion wafers because the consecrated ones were sinful to eat and would send you straight to hell, dried flowers pressed in books, wild daisies and clovers, candies, marbles of all colors and sizes everything to win her heart.

However, the story she remembered with the most joy was when Pepín invited her to climb the bell tower of the Basilica of Teror.

She remembered the altar boy had asked her to meet him in the town square shortly after ten in the morning, and as if he were about to give her a treasure, he said:

"Today, I'm going to take you to a place that few people know."

"Oh? And what place is that?" Angélica asked with great interest.

"The church bell tower. Only the important altar boys have the key, and we're the ones who ring the bell. No one else can do it, except the priest, of course, but he's always complaining that his knees hurt too much to climb the narrow stairs."

"The bell tower? Really? We're going to climb the bell tower, Pepín?" Angélica asked excitedly.

"Do you want to go? It's a magical place," he said, with the sparkle of a lover in his eyes.

"Of course, I want to go!" she replied enthusiastically.

Together, they crossed the square and headed toward the Basilica.

The bell tower rose to the left of the church's central entrance. Angélica found it impressive as she looked up to where the bell hung. The altar boy pulled out a large, old, rusty key, opened the door, and told her to follow him.

Pepín led the way, climbing some steps that were so small and close together that it made it difficult to reach the top of the tower. Angélica noticed a strong smell of dampness, as if the inside of the staircase had never been aired out.

After climbing the small steps for a while, they reached the top of the bell tower, and there Pepín showed her the panoramic views from the tower, a sight she had never had the chance to see, and she was impressed.

From above, Teror looked different. The houses were seen from another perspective, the white rooftops with clothes drying, the nearby mountain seemed greener, and the people looked like little toy soldiers walking along the cobbled streets.

Then Pepín explained the different bell tolls he had to ring: the prayer toll, the Sunday toll, the death toll, the feast day toll, etc.

Then, Angélica asked, intrigued:

"But how do you do it?"

"Look, you grab the rope, hold it tightly, and pull down, like this..." said the altar boy but without actually doing it.

"Oh, like this," Angélica said, grabbing the rope and pulling down with all her strength, and the bell instantly began to chime.

"But Angélica, what have you done? They're going to kill me. Let's run! The priest will skin me alive when he finds out," he said, terrified.

They ran down the stairs, stumbling, praying not to be caught, and fleeing the scene as quickly as possible.

When they reached the square, exhausted from running like mad, Pepín asked Angélica, frightened:

"What do I tell the priest now?"

"Tell him it was a stray pigeon or a wild cat," Angélica replied.

"Do you think he'll believe me?" he asked incredulously.

"Of course not, but who else would ring the bell at that time, a ghost?"

"Yeah, but that's lying, and if I say that, I'll be sinning," the altar boy said with a serious expression.

"If he asks, you tell him what I told you, and after a few days, you confess, and it's all settled. God will forgive you; it's a white lie," Angélica said, confident.

The next day, Pepín told her that the priest had asked why the bell had rung at ten twenty-five. He replied with what Angélica had told him, and the priest looked at him strangely but didn't give it much importance.

She closed the album, smiling as if closing a chapter of her life she would never live again. She got dressed and went to a hair salon specializing in alternative styles. She cut her hair in a military style, dyed it blonde, got a piercing on the left side of her lower lip, and another on her right nipple.

When she got home, her parents were startled by their daughter's new image. She looked at them as if asking what the problem was. Her father was the first to speak, angrily asking:

"What's with this look, Angélica?"

"What look are you talking about, Dad?" she said ironically.

"Don't mock me; you know exactly what I mean. I'm not in the mood for jokes."

"You were born angry, to put it mildly. Look, Dad, it's just a change of look. I was tired of the same old packaging all my life. It was time for a change."

"Well, just so you know, your mother and I don't like your appearance at all, because that's how other bad habits start that I don't want to discuss."

"The habit doesn't make the monk, Dad. There are many who wear suits and ties and are scumbags. They're everywhere out there. Don't think that just because I've changed my appearance, I'm going to become the city's number one criminal, be wanted, and end up drugged in a piss-filled corner. No, Dad, no. For the first time in my life, I've got my feet on solid ground; I know where I'm going. I don't think my image should matter to you or anyone else. It's my life, and I'll do with it what I think is right."

"Absolutely not, young lady! As long as you live under my roof, you'll do as I say. That way of dressing is not appropriate for a young lady, and I don't approve of it at all. You look like one of those crazy anti-system protesters on TV, throwing Molotov cocktails, throwing stones, and squatting in houses. What will the neighbors say!"

"If you want, I'll move out tomorrow. I'm sure I'd be happier living alone than putting up with your shouting and insults. And stop worrying about what the neighbors say. Do they feed you? Do they pay your salary? No, right? Then to hell with them all."

"That's not the point, Angélica! In life, appearances are very important; they're your business card, your introduction to society. But daughter, have you looked in a mirror? Do you think you'll be accepted for a job with that look? From the moment you walk in, they'll look you up and down and dismiss you, I guarantee it."

"I already told you I don't care what others say, and I don't need a job, I already have one," Angélica replied.

"You have a job? Where? It's not in some seedy dive where they sell drugs, drink themselves to death, and close at dawn, is it? And what about your studies?" her father asked irritably.

"No, Dad, it's not one of those jobs, although if I explain it to you, you'd never understand, so don't worry about it. What amazes me is that you're now worried about my studies, Dad, when you've completely ignored me. Do you even know what I'm studying? No, right? You have no idea what your daughter is studying."

"I have enough to deal with bringing home a paycheck so you can eat, dress, and study. You know I haven't been able to with the job I have; I work like a mule twelve hours a day to support this family and also take care of your studies. No one looked after me; I got ahead on my own without anyone's help, and here I am."

"Yes, Dad, yes, you always tell me the same story, but I exist, you know? But you've preferred to sit and eat your slice of TV in your daily sandwich, worry about what the neighbors say, and my virginity the rest, you couldn't care less."

"That's not true, but tell me, what's this job? Because some extra money would do us good," her father said.

"That's where you were heading, but don't worry, I've already given some money to Mom, and it seems she hasn't told you. I'm no longer your little girl; I've grown up and have a life ahead of me. Besides, don't try to live my life; it's impossible, and you'll end up badly. Sit in front of the TV with your remote and let the world spin around you," she said, heading to her room.

At that moment, her brother walked in and exclaimed when he saw her:

"Wow, Angi! What a radical change. You look amazing."

"Thanks, Richi, but it seems not everyone thinks so," Angélica said sadly.

"Who? The old folks?" he asked, glancing at their parents, "They're stuck in the Jurassic period, so don't worry; they gave me a hard time too, they're just old-fashioned."

"Yes, keep encouraging your sister, she looks like a tramp," her father scolded angrily.

"I'm not a tramp," Angélica retorted.

"But, old man, she looks super-hot, and it was about time she changed because she looked like a vampire and a prude."

"Don't overdo it, Richi," his sister scolded him. "Alright, enough, if you don't like it, don't look, I'm not changing."

"I hope this isn't the beginning of something you won't be able to control later," her father warned.

"Don't worry, Dad, I control my life, I've always had my feet on the ground, and now more than ever," she said to her father as she slammed her bedroom door.

When she was alone, she walked over to the full-length mirror in her wardrobe and looked at herself for a few minutes, feeling satisfied. She wondered if she really looked that different and why she seemed so repulsive to her parents.

She took off her black T-shirt and touched the steel cross on her right nipple. Then she took off her pants, standing completely naked in front of her mirror. She thought she needed some tattoos. The first would be a six-pointed star circling her navel, and the second, the name Quirina on the lower part of her back. Then she opened her wardrobe, took out a bag, and pulled out some black stretchy pants and a short-sleeved electric blue blouse, very tight and made of lycra.

When she was dressed, she looked at herself in the mirror again and admired her new, impressive look. She put on her black glasses and left her room. As she was heading out of the house, her brother Richard complimented her:

"Goodbye, gorgeous, you're going to take a big bite out of the world..."

She looked at him with a sly smile and flipped him the middle finger.

Meanwhile, her father muttered a series of curses to her mother, which she didn't clearly hear because she covered her ears with her index fingers.

Out on the street, she waited for a taxi. Shortly after, she saw one approaching, raised her hand, and whistled loudly until it stopped right beside her. Once she was seated, the taxi driver asked where she wanted to go, not hesitating to devour with his eyes the perfect breasts peeking through her lycra shirt in the rearview mirror.

"To Parque Santa Catalina, please."

"Okay," the taxi driver replied, not taking his eyes off his passenger.

"If you keep looking at me like that, we're going to have a nasty accident. So keep your eyes on the road because I don't want to die young," Angélica said sarcastically.

She didn't blame the taxi driver, who kept glancing at her out of the corner of his eye, but rather her appearance because society wasn't prepared to see a woman dressed like that. She was truly provocative, and that was the effect she wanted to have on people.

When they arrived at their destination, Angélica headed to the tattoo shop run by a Brit from Manchester.

The Englishman wasn't surprised by the look of his future client because he was used to seeing all kinds of eccentric characters in his shop, but he still looked her up and down.

She waited for him to finish with a guy who was getting a dragon tattoo that covered his entire back and was in his fourth session. When he finished with the dragon guy, the tattoo artist asked:

"What tattoo do you want to get? Here I have a series of models that might interest you."

"I brought my own designs. I want two: a star around my navel and a name on the lower back."

"Do you have the designs printed? If not, you'll have to draw them for me."

"Yes, I brought them printed so there wouldn't be any confusion," Angélica said.

"Let's see, show them to me so I can get an idea."

Angélica took them out of her backpack and handed them to him.

"Well, they don't seem very complicated; we'll finish up quickly. I'll charge you sixty euros for each one."

"Agreed," she said without arguing about the price.

When he was done, the Brit gave her a few tips on how to take care of them and recommended a cream for treating the tattoos.

By the time she got home, it was almost night. When she entered, her parents didn't say a word but followed her with an inquisitive look until she reached her room.

She took off her clothes, standing naked, and looked at herself in the mirror as she had that morning. She stopped to look at the tattoos. The star had turned out well, with red hues that faded as they approached the points, and the name Quirina was to her liking. She took a bit of the cream the tattoo artist had recommended, which she had bought at the pharmacy, and gently massaged it onto the affected area.

When she was done, she sat on the bed and saw the recent photo on the dresser, next to the picture of her cousins and grandfather. She looked at it carefully and then focused on the image reflected in the mirror. Everything had changed; she truly didn't recognize herself. Angélica was fading away like shadows at dawn, and there was no turning back.

She reflected on everything that was happening in her life. Not just the radical change she had made to her appearance but the irresistible feeling that was pushing her further and further, to become a completely different person from who she had been up until now. Every day, she was more aware that Angélica was giving way to Quirina. The avatar was winning the game, a game in which Angélica had been left in a corner waiting for her death.

She picked up the photo with her cousins and grandfather and smiled sadly because those times would never return. All she had left were the memories of a happy childhood.

She recalled the first time she visited the Finca de Osorio, located on the outskirts of Teror, which had gradually become a Nature Classroom where you could find a great diversity of flora and fauna.

They had gone to that magnificent place to capture lizards for her older cousin, Candela, who was collecting data for a thesis on the epilepsy of those Canary reptiles.

That day was an event because all the cousins went to the estate, escorted by Grandpa Juan, who had known the caretaker since he was a child and allowed them to spend the day near the mansion. The plan was to capture two or three lizards with buckets and tomatoes.

So they set up three buckets with open tomatoes inside, leaving a clear trail of tomatoes to lure the lizards in and trap them.

Meanwhile, all the cousins were jumping and running around the estate, playing hide-and-seek, handkerchief, spider-fist-cane, being careful not to damage anything to avoid bothering or explaining themselves to the caretaker.

At lunchtime, Grandpa pulled out some potato tortillas and soft drinks for everyone. When they finished eating, Grandpa asked:

"Do you want me to tell you the story of the living dead?"

"Yes, Grandpa, yes," all his grandchildren answered in unison.

"Are you sure? It's a scary story," he said, emphasizing the last word.

"Yes, Grandpa, yes...."

"Well, we arrived in Haiti right after the great war ended, in late 1945. A terrible hurricane from the South forced us to deviate from our route, which was Miami, and seek refuge on that Caribbean island. We had all heard the stories about zombies, as the Haitians called them, living dead to us. One night, our captain fell terribly ill with a terrible fever that made him jump out of bed. The doctors did everything they could to save his life, but by the next morning, he was as dry as a bone. His son, who was making his first trip with us, was devastated by the unexpected death of his father. We wanted to bury him, but his son said no, that there was still a chance to bring him back to life, and he asked us if we didn't know that in these lands, the dead were resurrected with voodoo magic. We tried to persuade him, but there was no way to make him see reason. So, when night fell, the captain's son arrived on our ship, followed by a retinue led by a voodoo witch doctor. They all went into the cabin where the captain's body lay, and we heard screams, chants in unrecognizable languages, and then silence.

"Following the witch doctor's instructions, the son told us we had to bury his father on solid ground and that he would return to life at dawn. We couldn't believe what he was saying, but we helped him bury our captain.

"The next morning, we accompanied the son to the grave, but everything was as it had been the night before. We went back for several days until we decided to set sail for Miami port."

"And that's it, Grandpa?" Angélica asked, disappointed.

"No, Angélica, no, because five years later, we returned to Haiti, this time without the captain's son, who never sailed again."

"And what happened, Grandpa?" Angélica asked.

"Well, when we went to the market to buy supplies to continue our journey to Europe, we found him."

"Who did you find, Grandpa? The captain?" they all shouted at the same time.

"Yes, but he was no longer our captain; he was a living dead man, a zombie who was the witch doctor's slave who had brought him back to life. The witch doctor tricked us all, especially the captain's son, who believed all his lies. Witch doctors often do this with the dead; they bring them back to life to turn them into their slaves."

"But that can't be, Grandpa. The dead are dead..." Angélica said.

"I don't know if it can be, Angélica, but I saw the captain as dead as a doornail and buried under three meters of earth. Then I saw him alive again; it's as true as I am here in front of you, telling you this story of a living dead man."

TRANSFIGURATION

All the grandchildren were amazed and believed every word their grandfather told them because he never lied. They got up, looking around for signs of a living dead man.

As evening fell and they were still frightened by Grandpa's fantastic tale, they went to check the buckets to see if they had caught any lizards in the traps.

They collected the buckets with no success until Angélica reached the last bucket, thinking there wouldn't be any lizards. But to her surprise, she found a huge one inside and, startled, dropped it and ran off, with the lizard running in the opposite direction. Cousin Candela's study would have to wait a few more days.

Angélica returned to the present, stood up, put the photo back in its place, and wondered if this transformation was due to some mental disorder, some type of paranoid schizophrenia that she couldn't clearly discern.

However, something inside her urged her to keep going as if she knew the path she had started on was the one she had to follow. Her avatar had shown it to her as clearly as daylight, and she had followed it without hesitation.

She put on the first T-shirt she found on top of the pile of clothes on her bed, sat in front of her computer, and activated her Second Life avatar. Instantly, she received a flood of messages from people wanting to talk to her, but she went straight to her office and put up a "Do Not Disturb" sign. A few minutes later, she received an instant message from her DJ, Arga.

"What do you want, Arga? I'm not in the mood to deal with anyone right now; I've had enough with that jerk Maliko, and I hope he doesn't come back here."

"Did something happen, Quirina?" Arga asked, concerned.

"He came to offer me a business deal that could be summed up as wanting to turn Quimera into a brothel. I told him no way, but the son of a bitch even threatened me. I already told you, I don't want to see him here, nor anyone who hangs out with him. You know who I'm talking about."

"Don't worry, boss, we've got them under control in our access program. If they want to enter, they'll have to create another profile and use another IP because both are monitored by our system."

"Alright, tell me, what brings you here? I don't have much time; my head is killing me, and I want to go to bed soon."

"It's something very important that could substantially change your life," Arga said, very interested.

"Tell me, I hope it's not a proposal like that stupid Maliko's. I have a hammer pounding in my head ever since I had that conversation with him."

"Okay, I'll be brief. There's a very influential person who wants to buy Quimera from you and is willing to pay a very reasonable amount."

"Damn! Yesterday pimps, today businessmen. I'm not selling Quimera. I now have direct contracts with many commercial brands that are paying me very well for their advertising. That's enough for me to live the life I want. I've found a goldmine, and I'm not selling it to the first person who offers me a reasonable amount."

"You should at least hear the amount he's offering. I think it's very interesting, and you should consider it."

"Arga, you know I respect you; you're a straight guy and one of the best DJs I've met, and I pay you well for it, but let me run my business."

"I know it's your business, but he's offering you 10,989,011 $L for it, which converts to thirty thousand euros."

"You know I'm making more than that annually," she said laconically.

"I know, but you're a smart woman, and you could start another club like this one and do just as well. You know how to do it; you have that talent that few people have for this kind of business, and wherever you go, you can count on me."

"I know I can count on you, Arga, but I'm not in the mood to think today. I've got a bipolar disorder that I want to resolve in the next few days," she said with heavy irony.

"Well, what do you think if we schedule a meeting for Saturday night? You don't lose anything by hearing his offer; if you don't like it, you can tell him to buzz off, and that's that."

"You're right, I lose nothing by hearing his offer. If I could put up with that jerk Maliko, this won't be worse. But Saturday is no good; I have plans. Friday at ten is better."

"Okay, I'll let him know. Think about it; I think it's a good opportunity."

"Fine, I'll think about it, but stop bugging me already," she said, annoyed.

She said goodbye to the DJ, took her avatar offline, and went to bed, turning over the offer she had received that very night in her mind. She couldn't believe it. In such a short time, she had gone from having no money in her account to depositing thousands almost daily, and now they wanted to buy Quimera from her. Everything seemed to be going too well to be real.

As she got up, she sat on her bed and saw her reflection in the mirror. At first, she was surprised; for a few seconds, she didn't recognize herself, as if her old personality had been stolen overnight. Who was that on the other side of the mirror?

It would take her a long time to adjust to her new face, her new life. It seemed that while she slept, Angélica reclaimed the body she lost at dawn, because she knew that from that moment on, Angélica ceased to exist and gave way to Quirina. She had spent many years living in a body that she now almost despised.

Regaining her awareness of who she was, she got up, took off her blouse, and removed the bandages from her two tattoos, exposing them to the light. She loved how the six-pointed golden star had turned out; it was looking great. She turned to see the name Quirina and also felt proud of how her other tattoo looked.

Who could she call to talk about this? She thought of her cousin Santiago, who was the oldest of them and had helped her a lot in choosing her major after finishing the entrance exams. She grabbed her cell phone and called him.

"Santi? Where are you?" she asked with interest.

"What's up, Angi? You've been more lost than Wally. How long has it been since we last saw each other?"

"I don't know, man. I've been really busy with something I want to tell you about."

"Speak up then," Santi replied.

"Not over the phone. I want to tell you in person, and that way, we can catch up because it's been ages since I've heard from you, and I want to know if you're still the same jerk as always, haha."

"Ugh, finally, love has knocked on your door..." he replied, not listening to her.

"Screw you. What love are you talking about? It's something more mundane than love."

"Okay, okay. When do you want to meet?"

"It's almost one. I'll treat you to lunch; you can choose."

"What? You're treating me to lunch? Santi, wake up; you're dreaming," he said, mocking her.

"I'm a businesswoman now, and I can afford these kinds of luxuries. So, what do you say? Do you accept my invitation?"

"A businesswoman? You never even had a place to crash before."

"I'm an entrepreneur with a bit of luck. But answer me, where do you want to go for lunch?"

"Well, how about the McDonald's on Triana?" he replied calmly.

"You and your junk food. You have no idea what real food is. This lunch is going to be cheap."

"Hey, no insults. Everyone has their tastes, and besides, you told me to choose, and I choose junk food, as you say."

"Alright, see you at one-thirty."

"Okay, beautiful."

"Bye, Santi, see you later," she said, ending the call.

Angélica sat for a moment, thinking about what clothes to wear, but she didn't hesitate for long. She grabbed her black pants and boots, a yellow T-shirt that exposed the two tattoos she had recently gotten, and left her room. Luckily, at that time, neither her father nor her mother was home, so she avoided another potential argument.

She checked her watch and realized she had time to catch the bus, so she walked to the stop just a few meters from her house. While waiting, she felt the prying eyes of some of the people there. When the bus arrived, she got on, and the driver gave her a look from head to toe, as if scanning her for a hidden bomb, especially around her chest, as she wasn't wearing a bra. Still stunned, the driver looked up at her face, and she lifted her black glasses, saying:

"My eyes are prettier, I assure you, even if you don't believe it," she commented with a mocking smile.

She walked to the back of the bus until she found a seat. From that vantage point and with the anonymity provided by her large dark glasses, she could see how most people were giving her furtive glances, scrutinizing every inch of her body. She had the urge to stand up and shout: "This is who I am, what the hell do you want?" But deep down, there were two things she was certain of: she liked dressing this way, and she loved disturbing the attention of those who looked at her. She felt different and powerful.

Before reaching her stop, she rang the bell while sticking out her tongue with a smile at a child no more than six years old, who kept staring at her as if she were from another planet, and got off at the Correos stop.

As usual, Primero de Mayo Street was packed with cars and people. She crossed without waiting for the light to turn green, under the watchful eye of a motorcycle cop who didn't take his eyes off her until she disappeared down Domingo J. Navarro Street.

When she reached Triana Street, she sat on the first bench she found near McDonald's to wait for her cousin Santiago, who always arrived late to most of his appointments. He said he had a hard time with physical-temporal calculations. But that day, his double interest in seeing his charming cousin and hearing her story made him more punctual than usual.

He walked past his cousin without realizing that the striking beauty sitting on the bench was Angélica. He stopped for a moment, looking around for any sign of his cousin. From the bench, she watched the scene with a suppressed smile and saw him pull out his phone and dial a number. After a few seconds, she heard, very close to where he was standing, the unmistakable ringtone of her cousin's phone, which was none other than one of the many marches of the Banda de Agaete. He turned around to where the ringtone, which he had heard countless times, was coming from, and realized the sound was coming from the girl sitting on the bench.

He observed her for a moment, then discreetly hung up the phone. He dialed the same number again, and once more, the Banda de Agaete's music came from the same spot.

Santiago didn't know what to think or do. So he hung up the phone, and the festival music stopped. The thought crossed his mind that this blonde with the shaved head had stolen or found Angi's phone.

Meanwhile, Angélica was enjoying her cousin's confusion. Without thinking twice, he turned towards the girl on the bench. Just as he was about to ask her about the phone, Angi pushed her glasses to the tip of her nose, revealing her stunning black eyes, and let out a hearty laugh.

"But... Angi?" Santiago managed to stammer, "What the hell have you done?"

"A radical makeover. I've wanted to do this for a while. Angélica is gone; now I'm Quirina," she declared firmly.

"Quirina? A makeover?! Ugh, too many surprises at once. You look like you've stepped out of a manga comic."

"Enough with the small talk. Give me a kiss. This isn't part of the story I want to tell you."

"Damn! Not part of the story? What do you want to tell me? Sorry, I'm overwhelmed. After years of seeing you as a quiet little mouse, suddenly, bam! You're a full-blown warrior. But whatever, you're still just as beautiful and just as hot. Come here and give me a hug," Santi said.

She stood up and, with a leap, hugged her cousin, nearly knocking him over from the impact. She kissed him on the lips and gave him a wink.

"Should we go inside, or should I get you some chamomile tea to help with the shock?" Angélica teased.

"Yes, let's go inside before I fall flat on my ass from the shock," her cousin replied.

They held hands like a couple and headed to a table at the fast-food restaurant.

"Aren't you aware that everyone is staring at you?"

"Of course, it's one of the consequences of my new look. But mostly, they're looking out of pure envy the girls because they want this amazing body, and the guys, well, you know why."

"How could they not stare? But have you looked in a mirror?"

"No, I go out like this every morning," she said sarcastically.

"Alright, enough stories, tell me what's going on. I'm all ears because there must be a reasonable explanation behind this transformation."

"Reasonable? I don't know if it's reasonable, but it does have an explanation."

"Then go ahead; I'm dying to know the details of your complex personality transformation. It's worthy of study."

"But first, go to the counter and get something because you know how they are," Angélica said, handing him twenty euros.

"Anything special?"

"Go to hell. You know what I want. I can't eat anything else in these places, you jerk."

"Damn! With that change, I thought you might have changed your eating habits too," he joked.

She momentarily dismissed him by flipping him the middle finger while her cousin blew her a kiss.

When he returned, he brought a chicken salad and a double cheeseburger with the accompanying drinks.

"Damn! Angélica exclaimed, "You haven't changed at all. Always stuffing twice the junk into your body. Do you know there are studies that say this food is a direct ticket to the grave?"

"Bahh, nonsense from advertisers with an agenda against this superfood."

"Super garbage, more like it. I know what I'm talking about," Angélica said firmly.

"Don't start with your philosophy now; get to the point."

"You know I've been chatting online since I was finishing high school and you were finishing engineering, if I remember correctly."

"Don't tell me you've fallen in love with some crazy guy, and you've changed because of him."

"And as you know," she continued, ignoring him completely, "I've been logging in ever since."

"I know, and I've been ignored all that time," her cousin complained.

"While I was completely ignoring you," she smiled, "I heard about Second Life and got interested in that virtual world, looking up information online, and soon after, I signed up under the name Quirina Muhindra. I spent a few weeks exploring that parallel world. I liked it so much that I couldn't go a night without logging in, walking its streets, and talking to all its people. But the strangest thing about all this is that the character I created for this world has gradually consumed what I used to be, as you can see."

"Angi? This is intense. Haven't you sought psychological help?" he asked seriously.

"I'm not crazy, Santi. For the first time in my life, I know what I want and how I want it. I'm very satisfied with my new image. But let me continue the story. So one day, I decided to become Quirina Muhindra, and this is the result. But that's not why you're here today."

"No? There's something stronger?" he asked, surprised.

"For me, this isn't anything intense; I've just tuned myself up a bit to impress passersby."

"Well, then get to the point; you've got me on edge," her cousin said.

"After living in SL for a few months, I decided to start a business, specifically a nightclub called Quimera. With some savings I had, I bought land and, with the help of some friends, set up the club. To cut a long story short, the nightclub has been a huge success in SL, and I'm making thousands of bucks a month."

"What? That's what I call luck. I've heard something about it, that a lot of money is circulating in Second Life and that even governments are trying to get involved because some mafias are using it to launder money from drugs, prostitution, and who knows what other shady businesses."

"Yes, Santi, you can make a lot of money if you have a good idea, dedicate enough time to it, and get a bit of luck. I've had all three, and now I have a business that's thriving."

"Okay, but where do I come in?" her cousin asked, looking for a reason why he was sitting there listening to his cousin.

"I want you to give me some financial advice."

"Me? But I have no idea about finances, remember? I'm an engineer; I work in industrial engineering, spending all day with the machines that make the world run. Economics is an unidentified entity to me, and I want nothing to do with it."

"But you're the only cousin I have who has a good head on his shoulders, and I trust you completely."

"Alright, tell me," he encouraged her, with a hint of uncertainty in his voice.

"Well, since Quimera is so successful, I've been offered 30,000 euros for the brand and the club," Angélica said.

"People are crazy. They've offered you that much for a virtual nightclub? Then it's true that a lot of money is being made in Second Life. Don't they need engineers?"

"No, no, people aren't crazy. I'm making two thousand euros every month, clear and free. It's a good business, but I need your advice because I don't know what to do. My intention is not to sell and keep the club unless the offer is irresistible."

"I think, first of all, you shouldn't part with the brand because you created it."

"Yeah, but the offer is very tempting, and I'm convinced it will go up a few thousand more."

"Perfect. Then I propose the following: First, accept the 30,000 euros as a lump sum for renting the brand and the club for five years plus 10% of the club's total profits."

"I agree with the first part, but the second is very difficult to control because how can I monitor how much Quimera makes to calculate that percentage? There's no way to know; they'll definitely screw me over."

"Then a fixed monthly fee, which could be between one thousand and fifteen hundred euros, because I suppose the buyer, if they're offering that amount, has seen a very interesting business opportunity."

"And you're the one who said you didn't know anything about finances?" she asked, astonished.

"Well, sometimes I surprise myself with my intelligence, but don't be fooled; it's all based on the unconsciousness of dozing off in front of the news and political-economic debates."

"It sounds like a good plan. See why it's important to have good advisors?"

"Especially good cousins, Angi. Advisors come and go, but good cousins, good friends, are always there, like park benches for you to sit on when you're tired or to share your sorrows and triumphs."

"Especially that, good cousins. If the deal goes well, I'll treat you to a meal at a decent place, not this multinational joint."

"But this is the food of the future..."

"Yeah, the future at this rate..."

"After talking business, let's talk about you because I'm still stunned by your transformation."

"What do you want me to say? I really like how I look. I've always seemed like a prude to others, and it seems that after a long time, I've found my true personality."

"Damn, it took you a while, and the change is, I don't know, a bit radical."

"You're right, it took a long time, but I spent most of my life studying and didn't have a moment to think about myself. It seems that by creating Quirina, something stirred inside me, and over time, I shaped her character, but at the same time, she was taking over mine until I realized that what I was up until that moment didn't appeal to me at all."

"I don't know, Angi. At first glance, it seems to me that Quirina has nothing to do with you."

"Look, I've only changed my outward appearance and added some spice to my personality."

"I hope that spice can be handled."

"Don't worry, everything is under control."

After finishing their meal and talking about this and that, Angélica said with a hint of irony:

"Well, handsome, I have to attend to my business online, but before I go, I want you to take a good look at my two tattoos, which I see your eyes keep lasciviously dropping to."

"No, woman, I'm just..."

"Don't justify yourself, just look and enjoy," Angi said as she lifted her short T-shirt.

"Nice star, and of course, Quirina couldn't be missing," he said, unable to take his eyes off his cousin's impressive body.

"Alright, that's it. Give me a kiss, and I'm off."

Her cousin watched her walk away for a few moments, like almost everyone else, unable to stop staring at his cousin. He wondered if this change would somehow affect their friendship because that was, in reality, the only thing that mattered to him at that moment.

When night fell, Angélica arrived home, and in the doorway, her smartphone rang with a call from an unknown number, but she didn't answer. The phone rang again instantly, and she hung up.

She wondered who was so insistently trying to talk to her. Soon after, she received a message telling her to answer the call because it was very important for her business. The phone rang again, and she asked:

"Who is this?"

"Miss Angélica, or should I call you Quirina?" asked a man with a strong Nordic accent but in perfect Spanish.

Hearing the nickname she used in Second Life, she knew Maliko had moved quickly and was aware of the offer to buy Quimera. Maliko had made good on his threats. She searched within herself for the strength needed not to lose her nerve and replied calmly:

"Yes, I'm Quirina; I don't discuss business over the phone."

"Any channel of communication is good when it comes to talking about money and business," the man on the other end replied.

"Our client," he continued, "is very interested in the club you have on the internet. We know there's an offer on the table from a very powerful bidder who will make you an offer you possibly can't refuse and that could be very lucrative. We don't know the amount you've been offered, but we'll double it, whatever it is. Our client wants your club at all costs, and we know you're willing to sell."

"Who told you I'm willing to sell Quimera? I haven't closed any deals with anyone, and selling isn't in my plans; it's going well, and it will continue to go well. That's why you're talking to me."

"Don't forget that everyone has a price, and so do you. There's a number that no one can refuse. However, we don't understand the ins and outs of the internet. We have orders, and we have to follow them. If you accept our offer, someone will contact you tomorrow; if not, we'll have to take more forceful measures. You understand me, right?"

Angélica's heart began to beat rapidly, and she remembered Maliko's words, that direct threat.

"You're a young, beautiful girl with a bright future ahead of you, and you have a rough diamond in your hands. You're faced with the dilemma of selling it or keeping it. If you sell it to the best offer, you'll make a lot of money in a short time and be set for the next ten years. But if you decide to keep it, they'll end up stealing it from you, and thefts usually involve a lot of violence, and you don't want violence, right?"

Angélica remained silent for more than a minute.

"There's no need to answer now. You're a very young woman with little experience in the business world, and you'll need advice before making such a significant decision. That's why we're giving you twenty-four hours to give us an answer. After that, if we don't get a positive response, we'll move to plan B, which I assure you, you won't like at all. You already know who to contact online to give us your answer; we won't call you again. Don't forget, we know exactly who you are, where you live, etcetera, etcetera. No need to explain, right?" said that sinister character.

"Yes, I know exactly what you mean, but that's no way to start negotiating the sale of a business. I don't like being threatened."

"It's just one way of negotiating. Understand, others use more subtle and less persuasive methods, but we use those that yield results. It's just a matter of efficiency and experience. We won't take up any more of your time. Remember, twenty-four hours, not a minute more, not a minute less. Say hello to your parents…"

Angélica was paralyzed for a few moments, not knowing what to do, while her heart tried to calm down from beating a thousand beats per minute. She couldn't believe what had just happened. The real world had knocked on her door.

She had been threatened directly, without any pretense or anesthesia; if she didn't sell Quimera, she would have problems, and from the tone of that character, the matter was dead serious.

They knew who she was, where she lived, and were willing to use violence to achieve their goals. Until that moment, she hadn't fully grasped the magnitude of the problem she was in. She didn't quite know what she was facing, but it didn't look good.

She entered her house and, without turning on any lights, went straight to her bedroom. In the solitude of her room, she stripped off her clothes and, once again, stood completely naked in front of the mirror, as if searching in her reflection for a path that would lead her to resolve her doubts, but she found no plausible answer.

On the table, she had two concrete offers for selling. One left no room for doubt: either she sold, or she would face problems of unknown magnitude, and the other was about to reveal its true nature.

She entered Quimera, activated the microphone, and called DJ Arga to meet with her in her office.

"Tell your contact that I want to speak with him," she said seriously.

"Has something happened, Quirina?"

"I'm not in the mood to explain. Just do me a favor and call your contact."

"Okay, he's waiting; it's already past ten."

"Then call him," she ordered.

Instantly, the businessman interested in buying her club appeared. His avatar was named Theodor Darvanlosky, an exclusive, registered, and purchased surname that no one else could use in Second Life.

He was as pretentious as one could imagine, a disjointed mix of Armani designs, Adolfo Domínguez, and others that were hard to identify.

"Good evening, Quirina. You have an attractive avatar; too bad I'm a one-track mind."

"The tracks on the internet are never clear; they may even converge."

"True, I spent most of my life thinking I was one way and eventually discovered I was another..."

"The same is happening to me, but we're not here to psychoanalyze ourselves, are we?"

"Absolutely right. I like that you get straight to the point. I hate it when people waste my time with nonsense. Now I understand why you've been so successful with this magnificent club. Succeeding in Second Life is no easy feat, my friend, and you've done it brilliantly. I congratulate you."

"Thanks, I appreciate it. But let's get to the point; I'd appreciate it."

"Let's get down to business. I imagine Arga has mentioned that I want Quimera. It's doing very well, and according to my analysts, it has a bright future with a few tweaks and some investment. I also know that others are interested in acquiring it. Those people are dangerous; they corrupt everything they touch and don't mess around when they want something."

Quirina remained silent for a moment, thinking about what Theodor was saying, still shaken by what had happened the previous night.

"From your silence, I sense they've already contacted you. According to my information, you're a young, brave woman with a bright future in this world. I have a lot of business experience, not just here but out there. I'm, let's say, a shark that smells good business from miles away, and yours is one. I've also been a victim of their threats, but the difference is that I have contacts both inside and outside Second Life, just like they do, and more than once, they've had to back down. Business is about power; you either have it, or you don't. The question is, do you want to sell Quimera?"

Quirina remained silent, listening intently to Theodor's explanations, unable to shake the metallic, threatening voice of that man from her mind.

"At the moment, I don't know; it all depends on the offer you make, but I don't want to give it up, no matter how much those bastards pressure me," Quirina confessed.

"I can offer you a reasonable price that meets your expectations."

"And what is that reasonable offer?" Quirina asked.

"I'm offering you 30,000 euros for your club."

"You know my club is worth double that. I have two proposals: the first, leasing Quimera for five years at 30,000 euros plus 2,000 monthly, and the second, 50,000, and you keep Quimera."

"We'll discard the first one; I want your club, and as for the second, don't you think you're pushing it a bit? With the information I have, you're not in a position to negotiate, Quirina. Those guys who talked to you are bad news; they'll do anything to get your club. I admit they've done me a favor..."

"They're offering me double what you are..." Quirina said.

"Yes, I know that story. They offer you double in three installments; they pay the first one, and the rest you'll have to chase down. That's how they operate; they're a mafia, don't forget that, Quirina. If you agree to sell, I'll deposit the agreed amount in one lump sum into the account you specify before signing the contract."

Quirina took a few moments to reflect on what Theodor had said, even considering the possibility that he might have orchestrated the entire threat strategy to scare her into selling Quimera at any price. But she wasn't willing to sell her business at a loss.

"Theodor, you have your advisors, and I have mine. I make 2,000 euros clean every month by dedicating three hours a day with minimal investment. If I put in a little more time and found an investor, I'd triple my income."

"True, but now an element has appeared that you didn't anticipate. You're alone in this business, my friend, alone in a world of sharks who've smelled your blood and are waiting for the right moment to devour you and leave you with nothing but bones. I'm offering you a dignified way out where you'll come out unscathed."

"50,000 euros seems like a reasonable price, and you know it. Quimera is worth much more."

"Let's see if we can close this deal in a way that benefits both of us. Let's make a compromise between your proposals. I'll offer you 45,000 euros plus 2,000 monthly for a year. What do you think?"

Quirina knew it was the best offer she could get at the moment because if she negotiated with those mafia types, she wouldn't have all the control, and if she didn't reach an agreement with Theodor, they would make her life impossible. She had no doubt about that.

"You don't happen to know Maliko, do you?" she asked openly.

"Hahaha, do you think I'm behind the threats you've received? DJ Arga has known me for many years; he worked with me before you came along and offered him the best job he's ever had. If you want references about me, just ask him. I'm a businessman, my dear, not a mobster."

"I was just considering the possibility. It's quite convenient that these people also want to buy my club," Quirina said.

"I'll confess something to you, my dear. Quimera has many suitors; you've only heard from two, but I'm the only one who's dared to take the step to make you an offer. The rest, knowing the others were interested, preferred to let it go; they don't want complications. But as I said, I'm an old shark with a lot of experience, and if anyone could make you another offer knowing the situation, it's me. So?"

"You've convinced me. I accept your offer, Theodor. I think under the current circumstances, I have no other choice."

"Perfect, but remember, you're a young and brilliant woman with a very promising future. When you have a great idea, which you will, look for me, and we'll figure out how to make it happen."

"One last thing..."

"But weren't you finished...?"

"You'll pay the commissions and handle all the paperwork with the SL administrators, and you'll keep the staff for at least a year."

"Of course, my dear, we'll also include that in the contract. I always say that when something works well, don't touch it because it will continue to work well."

"Deal closed, then?" Quirina asked with satisfaction.

"Completely closed; in a few days, Quimera will be mine."

"It's a pleasure to do business so quickly."

"You have the makings of a negotiator. My guys already have all the paperwork ready; it'll be settled between today and tomorrow."

"So you knew I'd sell," Quirina said.

"It was a possibility, and I never dismiss possibilities."

"Okay, Theodor. I hope to do business with you again someday."

"Don't doubt it, my dear, don't doubt it."

Angélica logged out of Second Life without saying goodbye to anyone and went to bed with the same thought that had been circling her mind since the night before. In the morning, she sat in front of her computer and saw an email from the SL administrators.

Theodor had moved quickly. She sensed he was eager to get his hands on Quimera and had a lot of influence. In the email, the SL admins sent her a link to a secure page with a username and password to access it. Within minutes, she had uploaded all her data, including her bank account. Once she had finished, they sent her a PDF document confirming the transaction.

Without wasting time, she opened a travel agency website and looked for the first ticket to Madrid and then to Sydney, Australia. She found a flight for that very night to Madrid and another for the following afternoon to Sydney, with a layover in London. She bought the tickets right then and there.

She grabbed her old camping backpack, packed some clothes and all her documents, and searched for her cell phone to call her cousin Santiago.

"What's up, Quirina?" her cousin joked.

"Can you take me to the airport this afternoon?"

"The airport? Where are you going?"

"To Australia."

"What are you talking about?" he asked, surprised.

"The deal went through; I sold Quimera, and I want to disappear for a while. Angélica and Quirina can't coexist in the same place, and I've decided that Angi has to die so Quirina can live."

"Angi, are you okay?"

"Let me explain clearly. Here and now, no one understands my change. I need to go to a new place and start a new life from scratch, and maybe I'll come back someday. Right now, I can't live in my parents' house because they don't understand my change. Living there has become unbearable. You know how my father is. He's the complete opposite of Grandpa Juan. If he were alive, he would have understood and supported me. My neighbors look at me like I'm a freak, my friends think I've lost my mind, and most importantly, I need time to digest this change, and I have to do it alone."

"You know I won't contradict you and that I support you, cousin. But couldn't you go somewhere closer, like El Hierro? You'd also be at peace, emerging from your cocoon."

"No, I need to go to a place where no one knows me. Sydney is a big, cosmopolitan, and open city. I won't feel out of place there, and I can start a new life," she said, confident.

"Well, I won't try to convince you. I think you've inherited Grandpa Juan's adventurous spirit from when he told us about his adventures in Venezuela and the Caribbean in Teror. Remember?"

"I remember it like it was yesterday, all of us gathered around him, listening to Grandpa's adventures, with that calm and deep voice and the tension with which he told his stories. Do you remember the zombie story? I was so scared, cousin. I still have nightmares..."

"Yeah, he was a master storyteller. He kept you on the edge of your seat until the end when, bam! He'd deliver the punchline, and we'd all jump half a meter off the ground in fright."

"Well, that's the way it is, Santi. I'm leaving with a one-way ticket, and I don't know when I'll be back."

"Have you told your parents?" he asked, worried.

"No, not yet, but I don't think I will. I'll leave them a note so they don't worry. Then my brother Richard can explain it to them in more detail. I don't want them to make a scene. I know my father well enough to know he'll find any reason not to let me go."

"Well, if Richi knows..."

"No, Richi doesn't know yet. I haven't told him anything; he's always been doing his own thing. He's a good brother, but he is who he is."

"So, everything's decided, Quirina?"

Angélica smiled upon hearing her avatar's name from her cousin's mouth for the second time.

"Everything, Santi. I just need you to take me to the airport this afternoon, and before that, I'll treat you to lunch at a good restaurant in Vegueta so you can remember me as the woman who introduced you to real food. What do you say?"

"Sounds like a great plan, but you don't need to take me to a fancy restaurant; a cheeseburger will do. Where should we meet?"

"At Plaza del Pilar Nuevo, at one-thirty. I'll let you go; I still have some things to sort out, and I don't know if I'll be able to get everything done in time."

"See you later, Angi... I mean, Quirina..." he said with a hint of unease.

As she left her room, she ran into her mother, who was cleaning the living room, giving her a cold, cutting look. She knew her transformation had hurt her mother in some way, but there was nothing she could do. Angélica sensed the discomfort her mother felt in her presence, a feeling that stabbed her heart like a red-hot knife.

Her mother had always followed her father's lead, saying and doing what he wanted, and never minded, perhaps because she had been taught from a young age that a woman's role was to serve the man. But Angélica disagreed entirely with that thought, which seemed outdated and obsolete to her, though many women, even in the twenty-first century, still thought and acted the same way.

Many times, she had tried to talk to her mother about it, but she would always say that things had always been this way and would continue to be, that she was from another time and not like now, when women were everything but housewives; without a doubt, times had changed.

She wanted to say something, to say goodbye, to give her a hug, but it wasn't worth it. Her mother no longer recognized her as her daughter. It would take a long time for that, for the open wounds to heal, and for everything to return to normal.

"Goodbye, Mom..."

Her mother looked at her as if she hadn't heard and continued with her chores.

She returned to her room, grabbed her backpack, and left the house without saying goodbye to her mother. At that moment, she dismissed the idea of leaving a note for her parents; her brother could explain the reason for her departure.

As she walked, she couldn't stop the tears from coming, tears seasoned with sadness and anger. She clenched her teeth to resist the urge to scream and cry for leaving behind almost everything that had been her life until then, and she succeeded.

She hailed the first taxi she saw and went to her brother's workplace, the first stable job he had at thirty-three. She didn't want to leave without saying goodbye to him because, although they hadn't shared much as siblings, he had always treated her with great affection, defended her, respected her, and supported all her decisions.

She got out of the taxi and went straight to the counter of the post office where her brother worked. When he saw her, he was surprised and thought something was wrong. It was the first time in all the time he had been working there that his sister had shown up at his workplace. So he signaled a colleague to cover for him and went to where she was.

"What's up, Angi?" he asked with a worried look.

"Nothing, Richi, don't worry," she said sadly.

"But you're here for a reason," he said, seriously.

"Yes, there's a reason, but it's nothing serious; no one has died, and I'm not pregnant…"

"Then, Angi?"

"I'm here to say goodbye."

"Goodbye?"

"I'm leaving for Australia this afternoon," Angélica said, trying not to cry.

"To Australia? Just like that? But why? Is it because of the trouble with the folks…"?

"Partly, yes. I can't live at home anymore, Richi. The situation is unbearable; I can't stand Dad's sexist and derogatory comments anymore, and Mom doesn't support me either. I need a change of scenery."

"Damn! Then go to Fuerteventura, but not Australia," he said, irritated.

"That's the same thing our cousin Santi said, but the decision is made, Richi, there's no turning back."

TRANSFIGURATION

"And what will you live on? Going to Australia requires a lot of money; the cost of living is very high; you need a lot of cash to survive."

"I don't lack money; I have enough for a couple of years, although I'll soon start working."

"And where did you get the money, Angi?"

"I started an online business on a platform called Second Life, and it went very well. Yesterday I sold it at a good price."

"An online business?" her brother asked, astonished. "No wonder you spent hours in front of the computer, and I thought you were wasting your time. Damn, you're something else, sis."

"That's it, brother. You'll have to get up to speed with computers and the internet to talk to me. I've left you all my equipment; it's almost new. I've also left some money for the folks and some for you. There are two envelopes in the top drawer of my console. I'd like you to try to explain to Dad and Mom why I left. Just tell them I was offered a good job in Sydney and not much else; I don't want them to feel guilty, okay?"

"I'm going to miss you, sis. Although we never had that perfect sibling relationship, you know I love you a lot, and if you need anything or can't stand the Aussies, come back to the Canaries. You know it's the best place in the world to live; we're the Fortunate Isles," her brother said with tears in his eyes.

"Don't worry, Richi. I'll be fine. I've got almost everything under control; with money in your pocket, things are easier, and besides, I've always been good at English. Come on, give me a hug. It's going to be a long time before we can do this again. And I have to hurry because our cousin Santiago is waiting for me."

They embraced tightly, and neither could hold back their tears. Angélica because she knew it would be a long time before she saw her brother again, and Ricardo because the emotion and incomprehension of the moment overwhelmed him.

She kissed him and quickly left without looking back. She paused for a moment, trying to hold onto the image of her brother in her memory, and as she did, a fraternal smile appeared on her face.

Shortly after, she raised her hand, and another taxi stopped beside her. She got in and told the driver to take her to Plaza del Pilar Nuevo, the penultimate stop on her journey toward an uncertain destiny. A destiny she had chosen with full awareness of what she was doing. A long road that would allow her to leave behind the remnants of Angélica's skin, already fading in her memories.

When she arrived at Plaza del Pilar Nuevo in Vegueta, she sat down to wait for her cousin, who, as always, was late.

The sound of the water relaxed her, and she remembered her grandfather Juan, who, like her, had left for distant lands barely twenty years old. She recalled the story her grandfather had told her more than once about how his first journey to Venezuela had been.

"I went down to Las Palmas because here in Teror, times were tough. After the Civil War, things were bad everywhere; there wasn't enough food for everyone. We managed because my father had a small garden behind the house, some chickens, two goats, and a mule, and with that, we got by.

"When I arrived in Las Palmas, things weren't much better. Like in the village, people in the capital were also suffering from the hardships brought by that damned war. I asked around everywhere for work, but there was no way to find a decent job for a young man like me.

TRANSFIGURATION

"While walking, I heard that the English were hiring workers at the dock, looking for laborers to load and unload their ships. I walked as fast as I could, even ran, not wanting to miss such an opportunity to earn a decent wage to help my family. However, when I arrived, the quota of laborers was full. Sadness overcame me as I wandered the Santa Catalina dock, desolate because I hadn't found the work I was looking for. After a while of walking around the dock, I stumbled upon some sailors loading a ship with supplies, and I asked if I could help in exchange for some coins. The man who seemed to be the captain looked me up and down and said yes, he couldn't pay me much, but they were in a hurry to finish loading the ship with provisions because they were sailing to America at sunset.

"I worked like a mule, loading all kinds of goods: crates of oranges, bunches of green bananas, salted fish, water, crates of lemons, and a bunch of other things. When I finished, the captain gave me what we had agreed upon and said:

'You're a good worker; I could use someone like you on this voyage, but few are prepared to leave this island.'

"Without thinking twice, I said:

'I'd be willing. I'm a country man used to hard work.'

'Then it's settled; if you want, you can sign on right now. You have a lot to learn, but you seem like a man eager to take on the world, and I need hard-working people.'

"Without thinking much about what I was doing, I boarded that ship bound for a part of America I didn't know. When we were at sea, I found out we were heading to Venezuela.

"For a few months, my parents thought I was dead until they received the first letter telling them I was fine and would return soon.

"And that's what I did. After ten years of sailing around the world, I returned to my land with my pockets full of hopes and money. I was finally able to help my family as much as I could. We bought land, goats, chickens, and built this house, one of the biggest in the village, because we were a large family.

"From that moment on, we never wanted for anything again, and I never had to go back to sea."

Her cousin Santi's voice snapped her out of her daydream.

"Angi? Angi? What's up? You seem stunned."

"Nothing, I was remembering Grandpa Juan's story. Do you remember when he told us about going to the Americas without telling his parents?"

"Of course I remember, and it reminds me of someone..."

"What I'm doing is different, Santi. I've already talked to my brother, and he'll explain everything to my parents."

"Your father will never forgive you..."

"I know, but he has to live his life, and I have to live mine. Our paths have separated for a while, and as they say, time heals all wounds. I think I'm doing the right thing for my future as a woman and as a person. If someone doesn't understand that, it's not my problem; I have to follow my path."

"I get it, Angi, but you have to understand that your decision is radical. I don't even understand it, let alone your parents, who are set in their ways..."

"I'm not asking you to understand; I'm just asking you to accept me for who I am, nothing more," Angélica said.

"Okay... let's go; I'm hungry. What's this great place you're taking me to for lunch?"

"It's not far; we can walk, but I assure you, you won't regret it."

TRANSFIGURATION

"If it beats a double cheeseburger..." her cousin said with irony.

After lunch, her cousin Santiago said the food was excellent and that it definitely beat the double cheeseburger.

They headed to the car, and during the drive to the airport, they talked little, only about trivial things. When they arrived, her cousin hugged her and said:

"Write when you get there..."

"As soon as I'm settled, I'll send you an email, and we'll talk on Skype. Please help Richi learn how to use it. I've left everything ready for him."

"Don't worry about it; he'll learn, though we know your brother is stubborn, but he'll get the hang of it. Don't worry," her cousin assured her.

"Well, this is where we part, cousin. I have to go; give me a hug because it'll be a long time before we can do this again."

The two cousins embraced tightly and said their goodbyes.

Angélica passed through security with all eyes on her, both from the security agents and the civil guards.

When the plane took off toward Madrid, Gran Canaria faded into the distance until it disappeared from view. She tried to sleep, thinking about the future awaiting her in Australia, and couldn't help but feel a bit of unease about everything that lay ahead.

However, she closed her eyes and began to recall Grandpa Juan's stories, her summer games in the square in Teror, her adventures in Finca de Osorio, her games with Pepín in the bell tower, her transformation, until she fell asleep.

She had already started to change her life and was convinced there was no turning back.

Also by Moisés Morán Vega

Cóctel de Microhistorias terrenales
El origen competitivo de los botes de Vela Latina Una aproximación histórica
Alí el Canario. Un corsario berberisco
Medio minuto para morir
Saduj. Caso I
No sin agua
Salvar al lagarto Tamarán. La culebra californiana
Poemas del ayer
Evolución deportiva e histórica de los botes de vela latina en Las Palmas de Gran Canaria: 1876-1962
Saduj. Caso II. Internos
Caminar hacia la salud
Teatro reunido
Ali the Canary. A Barbary corsair
My facebook after death
K-70. The adventures of a majorera turtle
Transfiguration

Watch for more at
https://elpatiodeloscangrejos.blogspot.com/.

About the Author

BiografíaMoisés Morán Vega nació en Las Palmas de Gran Canaria el 20 de junio de 1965, en el barrio de Escaleritas.Ingresa en la Facultad de Educación Física y Deportes, donde se doctora en Educación Física con la tesis Análisis praxiológico de la situación motriz en competición de los botes de vela latina en Las Palmas de Gran Canaria (ULPGC 2005) y, posteriormente, cursa el Máster en Gestión Deportiva por la Universidad de Las Palmas de Gran Canaria.En el año 2007 se vuelve a interesar por la escritura de forma intensiva, escribiendo en su blog poesías, microrrelatos y relatos de diversa temática. Dos años más tarde, en el año 2009 gana el Primer Premio de Narrativa Breve Episodios Insulares convocado por la editorial Cam-PDS con el cuento juvenil, La Sima.En la actualidad es funcionario de la Comunidad Autónoma de Canarias y miembro activo de la Asociación Canaria para la Edición (NACE).BibliografíaNovelaHistorias de un esquizofrénico que no quería serlo, pero que lo era, 2010.Chat, 2013.Conexión Jinámar, 2014.Medio minuto para morir, 2015Alí el Canario, 2015Saduj. Caso I 2016Narrativa infantil y juvenilLa Sima, 2011 (Relato ganador del primer Premio de Narrativa Breve Episodios Insulares convocados por la editorial Cam-Pds en año 2009).Ali Romero. La historia de un corsario berberisco, 2011.Víctor, el caracol con un solo cuerno al Sol, 2012.Rocky y las tres cucarachas, 2012.El alambre mágico, 2013.Salvar al lagarto Tamarán: 2014.K-70: Las aventuras de una tortuga majorera, 2014.Alí el Canario. Un corsario berberisco. 2015Teatro"Gracias por su visita", 2015"Ganar, ganar", 2015"El testamento", 2015

Read more at https://elpatiodeloscangrejos.blogspot.com/.

www.ingramcontent.com/pod-product-compliance
Lightning Source LLC
Chambersburg PA
CBHW060505160726
47992CB00003B/1344